Pop and Len

by Susan Hartley • illustrated by Anita DuFalla

"Can I go in the lab, Sam?" said Len.

"No, Len. I cannot let you go in the lab," said Sam.

"Let the lad go in the lab, Sam," said Pop.

"Can I sit on a lap?"
said Len.
Pam said, "No, Len.
You cannot sit on my lap."

"Let the lad sit, Pam," said Pop.

"I can see the cat in the rug," said Len. "I can lug the cat with the rug."

"No!" said Pop.
"You cannot lug the cat.
You cannot go in the lab.
You cannot sit on a lap."

"But you can sit with me!" said Pop.